The three Billy Goats Gruff lived on a farm at the bottom of a mountain.

Every morning, the three Billy Goats Gruff ran up the side of the mountain to go and graze, but they had to stop when they got to the river.

In the river, there was an ugly old troll who lived under some wooden planks. The troll was angry all the time and he never let the three Billy Goats Gruff cross the river.

The troll yelled and shouted if the three Billy Goats Gruff went too close to his wooden planks. Whenever an animal tried to cross the planks, the troll jumped up and flashed his long, sharp teeth.

The three Billy Goats Gruff looked longingly at the bank on the far side of the river.

"If only we can get across the river, we can go to the top of the mountain. There is a lot more food on that side of the river," said the biggest Billy Goat Gruff.

"Come along, then," said the smallest Billy Goat Gruff. "I bet I can run across so quickly that the troll will not see me."

The biggest Billy Goat Gruff tried to stop him, but the smallest Billy Goat Gruff started running. Trip, trap, trip, trap went his hooves on the wooden planks.

The ugly old troll started to roar and shout when the smallest Billy Goat Gruff set off across the planks.

"GET OFF MY PLANKS!" he roared. "You cannot cross the river. I will chomp you and munch you up for dinner," and he snapped his long, sharp teeth at the smallest Billy Goat Gruff.

The smallest Billy Goat Gruff was so afraid that he started to shake. "Do not munch me up for dinner!" he cried. "I am too small to make a good dinner for a big troll like you. A much bigger billy goat will come by in a little while."

"Hmm, you are quite small," muttered the troll, rubbing his chin and looking at the next goat. As he did so, the smallest Billy Goat Gruff slipped quickly across the planks.

The second Billy Goat Gruff said,
"If the smallest Billy Goat Gruff can get across the river, then so can I!"
He started to run across the wooden planks - trip, trap, trip, trap went his hooves.

Up jumped the troll again, shouting.
"Mmmm! DINNER!" he cried, and rubbed his belly. "I like goat for dinner," he smiled.

The second Billy Goat Gruff waited for the troll to finish shouting.
Then he said, "Do not have me for dinner. I am too small to make much of a dinner for a big troll like you. The biggest Billy Goat Gruff will come by soon, and he will make a much better dinner for a troll of your size."

"Mmmm," said the troll, rubbing his chin and licking his lips as he looked across at the biggest Billy Goat Gruff.
As he did so, the second Billy Goat Gruff ran quickly across the planks.

As the biggest Billy Goat Gruff came along, the troll yelled and stamped and shook his fists.

"I shall munch you and chomp you and have you for my dinner!" he shouted, and smiled so that the sun shone on all his big, sharp teeth.

“NO, YOU WILL NOT!” shouted the biggest Billy Goat Gruff, and he snorted and stamped his hooves. He shook his horns at the troll and then started to run. TRIP, TRAP, TRIP, TRAP went his heavy hooves on the wooden planks.

The troll shouted and stamped and gnashed his teeth. The biggest Billy Goat Gruff snorted and ran at the troll. His big hard horns butted into the troll, who went spinning up and up and up, and then...

SPLASH! The troll landed in the river. He bobbed up again and spluttered as he tried to shout, but the river swept him off. He waved his arms and shook his fists as he was dragged around a bend in the river.

The biggest Billy Goat Gruff ran safely across the planks. All three Billy Goats Gruff were so glad that the troll had gone that they jumped about.
"You were so brave!" cried the smallest Billy Goat Gruff, hugging the biggest one, and the three goats ran happily on, up to the top of the mountain.

As for the troll, he was never seen on that mountain again. He found a dark cave in some rocks where he made his home, and he never stamped and shouted or tried to have goat for dinner again.